Pet Lizard

by Stef Schumacher

illustrated by Tom Leonard

Orlando   Boston   Dallas   Chicago   San Diego

Visit *The Learning Site!*

www.harcourtschool.com

Tina liked lizards. For a long time she had wanted to have a lizard for a pet. Some of Tina's friends wanted a kitten or a puppy or a goldfish, but Tina wanted a lizard. She knew that some lizards were green and smooth and that others were brown and bumpy. Some lizards had big eyes, and others had really long tails. Tina liked them all.

Tina's mom said having a lizard for a pet would be a big responsibility. Lizards need special care and attention because they are very sensitive animals. Tina agreed heartily.

Tina knew that part of being a good pet owner was choosing the right pet. There were so many lizards to choose from in all different sizes and colors. Each lizard had its own special needs. Which lizard was the right one for her?

Tina knew it would be best to do some research before choosing. So she decided to turn this search for the perfect lizard into a project. First, she would collect all of the information she could find. Then, she would study it. Finally, she would make her decision. That way, she could be sure that her decision would be the best one.

Here's what Tina learned from her research.

Komodo Dragon
Komodo dragons grow to be about 5 feet long. They like to swim in the ocean and eat seaweed. Komodo dragons also like to lie in the sun on volcanic rocks to get warm. Because they are cold-blooded animals, Komodo dragons need the sun to keep warm. If the Komodo dragon gets too cold, it can't move.

The Komodo dragon likes to hunt big animals, such as deer. Its tongue is a foot long! When a dragon smells the air with its sensitive tongue, it can tell in which direction to look for food.

Basilisk Lizard

Basilisk lizards are found near ponds and rivers. They have very long hind legs and are fast runners. In fact, they are so fast that they can run on water.

Some people are afraid of basilisks. They think a basilisk brings bad luck if it looks you in the eye!

Basilisk lizards are found in Mexico and South America. They live in shrubs and trees, along with other small animals that the basilisks eat. Basilisk lizards also eat the fruit that grows on the bushes and trees.

Jackson's Chameleon

Jackson's chameleons have long tongues that they shoot out very far to catch their prey. Their tongues are sticky on the end, which helps them catch insects. The tongue of the Jackson's chameleon is one and a half times as long as its body. That's a very long tongue! Most of these chameleons live in Africa. However, many also live in Hawaii, where there are lots of plants and rain.

You can tell which Jackson's chameleons are male and which are female because only the males have three horns on their heads. Males and females both have long tongues for catching insects.

African Chameleon

The African chameleon likes to live in dry forests and savannas, which are found in many parts of Africa. Hiding among plants, these chameleons change color with their surroundings. Depending on where they are, African chameleons can be green, brown, or yellow. African chameleons also have interesting eyes. They can move one eye forward and the other eye backward at the same time!

Can you imagine having eyes like an African chameleon? How do you think the world might look? It might be fun to be able to see in two directions at once.

Leopard Gecko

When the leopard gecko is a baby, it has stripes. As it grows, the stripes fade into a pattern of spots, just like a leopard!

It's not a good idea to pick up a gecko by its tail. The gecko will get scared and try to get away. Then its tail will break off. Later, the gecko will grow a new tail in place of the old one.

Tiny scales cover the pads of the gecko's feet and enable it to grip smooth surfaces. The leopard gecko can climb on glass or almost anywhere!

Most pet owners like geckos because geckos tend to like people.

After Tina gathered lots of information about lizards, she studied it all very carefully. She hadn't known there was so much to learn about them. Now she knew a lot about several different kinds of lizards.

She decided to make a list of all of the lizards she had researched. She thought about each lizard on the list and its special needs. The first name she crossed out was the Komodo dragon. That lizard would just be too big for her small room. Komodo dragons also like to live near the ocean. Tina couldn't fit the ocean into her room! The next name she crossed off was the basilisk lizard, which needs a big area where it can run. Definitely not a good choice for a bedroom!

Then Tina crossed out the African chameleon and the Jackson's chameleon, because both of these lizards need to be surrounded by plants. Although she liked plants, Tina wasn't sure she would have time to take care of plants *and* a lizard.

Now there was just one lizard left: the leopard gecko, a small, friendly creature. Tina had found her perfect pet! She rushed off to tell her mother.

"When can we get it?" Tina asked. She was very excited. "Can we go now?"

Tina's mother was sitting at her computer, working on a recipe book she was writing. "I'm afraid I'm too busy to go right now," her mother answered. "You did a great job researching the subject, though, Tina. I promise we'll go to the pet store together this weekend."

Although Tina loathed the idea of waiting, she was happy her mother was willing to help her find the perfect pet.

Tina and her mother agreed to pick out the new pet together. There were many lizards at the pet store, but they finally found a leopard gecko they both liked.

The two of them agreed with certainty that this was the best gecko in the pet store. It was just the right size for Tina's room, and it would be a friendly pet. Tina already knew all about how to care for it, too. This gecko seemed like the right pet for her!

"What will you name it?" asked Mom.

"I'm going to call it Soda!" said Tina.

Then they selected a cage that would make her leopard gecko feel at home.

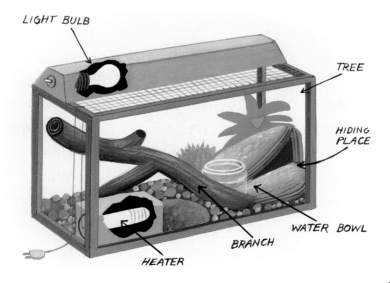

LIGHT BULB

TREE

HIDING PLACE

WATER BOWL

BRANCH

HEATER

They brought the gecko and its cage home.
Tina knew the gecko would need sunlight, even
on a cloudy day, so she put a special light bulb in
the cage that produced light like the sun's. Tina
also put a small heater in the cage to keep her
gecko warm. Since the heater protruded into the
cage, Tina put a protective covering over it.

Her gecko would need places to hide and rest.
Sometimes geckos get nervous. A hiding place
lets them feel safer and rest. In the wild, all
animals have hiding places. Tina knew that a
good pet owner is never indifferent to the needs
of her pet.

"It looks like it might be hungry," said Mom.

"Here goes!" said Tina.

She dropped a live cricket into Soda's cage. Live crickets are one of the leopard gecko's favorite foods. Gulp! Soda gobbled the cricket up.

"Yuck," said Tina.

"I bet Soda thinks yum," said Mom.

Undoubtedly, thought Tina. She was going to have to get used to feeding Soda. She knew it was important to take good care of her pet, and she never wanted Soda to be hungry. Tina knew that feeding crickets to Soda was an important responsibility.

Tina and her mother were so busy feeding Soda that they didn't notice that the crickets had gotten out of the bag. There were crickets everywhere! Her mother said, "Please, Tina, help me find them!"

Two hours later, Tina and her mother thought they had rounded up all the crickets. It was a wild start, but day by day, Tina got used to taking care of her pet gecko.

One day she was playing with Soda. "Look at the lizard, Soda," Tina said. She held up a toy basilisk lizard she had bought for Soda to play with. Soda seemed indifferent to it. Tina wasn't sure what to do.

"I think Soda's lonely," Tina announced to her mother. "I can't exactly explain it, but he seems to be acting kind of sulky lately."

"What makes you think so?" her mother asked.

"Well, he doesn't seem interested in the toy lizard I bought for him. Maybe he needs a real, live friend," Tina answered.

"I'm not sure that a leopard gecko really has those kinds of feelings," her mother said. Then she thought for a minute. "Just in case you're right, though, you can get another lizard. You've been so good about taking care of this one that I trust you to have two geckos."

15

Tina gave her mother a hug. "You won't be sorry," she promised.

"Taking care of two lizards is a big responsibility," her mother reminded her. "That means two lizards to feed."

"I know," Tina said, "but I can handle it, Mom. I don't want Soda to be lonely."

"Soda's going to have two good friends then," said Mom.

"Two?" asked Tina.

"You and a new gecko!" said Mom. "What will you call the new gecko?"

"I'm going to call it Pop!" said Tina. "Soda and Pop!"